This Orchard
book belongs to

_____

_____

_____

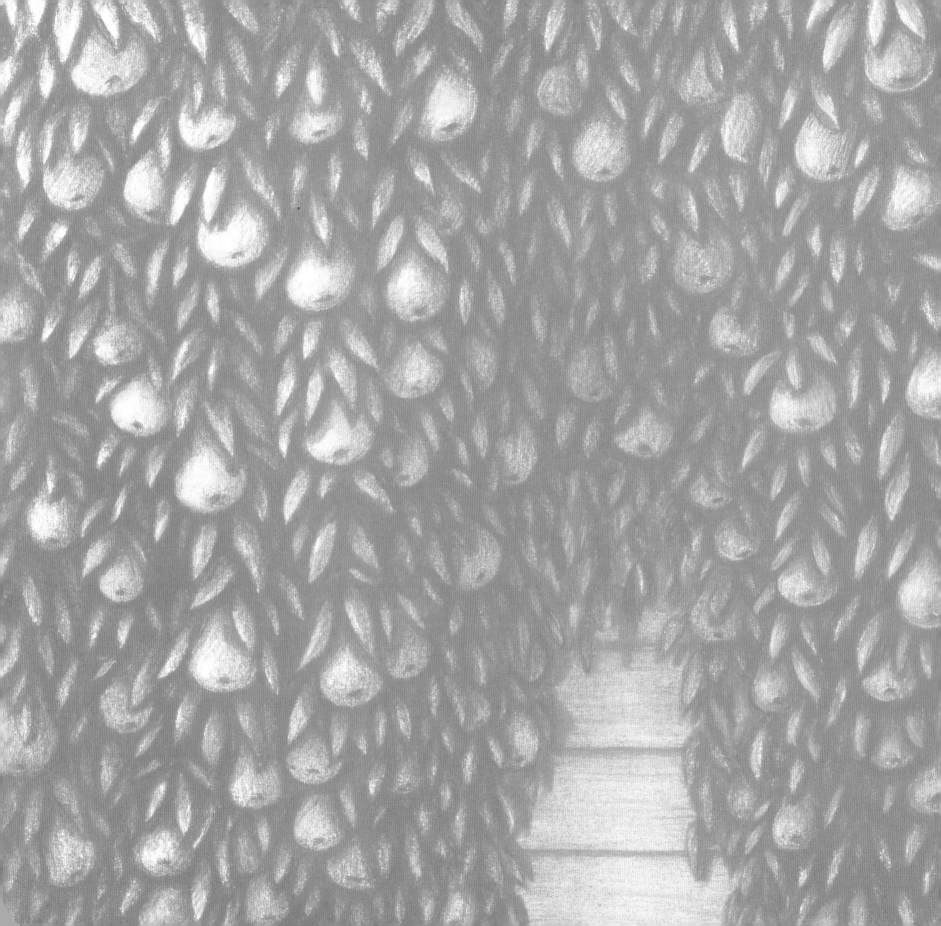

To Ann-Janine, Richard, Conrad and Enzo
with our warmest wishes, T.M. & P.H.

ORCHARD BOOKS

338 Euston Road, London NW1 3BH
Orchard Books Australia
Level 17/207 Kent Street, Sydney, NSW 2000

First published in 2008 by Orchard Books
First paperback publication in 2009

ISBN 978 1 84616 246 6

Text © Tony Mitton 2008
Illustrations © Paul Howard 2008

A CIP catalogue record for this book is available from the British Library.

10 9 8 7 6 5 4 3 2 1

Printed in China

Orchard Books is a division of Hachette Children's Books, an Hachette UK company.
www.hachette.co.uk

A Very Curious Bear

Tony Mitton & Paul Howard

ORCHARD BOOKS

These are the words that a little bear said
with a blink and a yawn as he got out of bed:

Why does the sun come and light up the day?
To wake you from sleep so you come out and play.

Why does the wind rush around in the air?
To fill you with joy and to blow away care.

And maybe to tease you by ruffling your hair!

Why does the path make such wriggles and bends?
To show us our journey and lead us to friends.

Why does the stream seem to gurgle and babble?
It's chuckling, "Dip in your toes for a dabble."

Why do the daisies squeeze up from the grass?
To drink in the light as the dreamy days pass.

Why does the rain come and wet the world through?
To help grow the things that we need to feed you.

Why does the sky go all rumbly with thunder?
To give *us* a shiver and fill *us* with wonder.

But why must the world fill with roaring and crashing?
It's the song of the storm, and the lightning flashing.

Why would the wind and the weather above
destroy such a beautiful thing that we love?

Bad things can happen which also bring good.
Just look, there's a bridge where the old tree once stood.

But the sun's going down and the world's turning grey.
Let's try to be home by the end of the day.

Why is the moon like a lamp in the sky?
For light and for beauty, and wondering why.

But what am I meant for and why am I here?
To live and to wonder, my darling, my dear.

Where do I go when I've fallen asleep?
To a place that is peaceful and dreamy and deep.

Then the curious bear gave a tired little yawn,
snuggled warmly in bed and slept softly till dawn.